The Walt Disney Family Museum

THE MAN, THE MAGIC, THE MEMORIES

Printed in the United States of America

First Edition

10 9 8 7 6 5 4 3 2 1

Reinforced binding

Library of Congress Cataloging-in-Publication Data on file.

ISBN 978-1-4231-2748-2

All works illustrated in this book are from the collection of the Walt Disney Family Foundation except for the following: Pages 10, 12-14, 16 (upper left), 17, 18, 20, 22-23, 32 (center), 34-35, 43 (center left and upper right), 51 (upper left), 56, 69 (upper left and lower right), 70 (top left and bottom left), 75 (lower left), 77-79, 81 (lower right), 83, 84 (top left), 85 (top right), 86-87, 92 (top), and 93 courtesy The Walt Disney Company, ©Disney Enterprises, Inc. Page 57 (top) courtesy David Lesjak. Page 90 illustration by Karl Hubenthal ©1966 Estate of Karl Hubenthal. Page 92 (top) illustration by R. A. Lewis ©1966 Milwaukee Journal Sentinel. Page 93 illustration by Gene Basset ©1966 Gene Basset.

The Walt Disney Family Museum gratefully acknowledges the generous cooperation of The Walt Disney Company.

Design: Em Dash
Writer: J. B. Kaufman

Chapter Title Illustrations

page 6: Shirley Temple presents Walt Disney with the special Academy Award® for Snow White and the Seven Dwarfs: one full-size Oscar® and seven little ones.

page 8: Walt Disney in his office at the studio, 1930s.

page 10: Walt Disney at nine months.

page 20: Walt, Lilly, and their pet chow, Sunnee, early 1930s.

page 28: The Disney studio transferred distribution of its cartoons to RKO Radio Pictures in 1937.

page 38: Sheet-music cover from Snow White and the Seven Dwarfs.

page 46: Story sketch from Pinocchio.

page 54: Striking Disney artists applied their talents to the making of strike propaganda.

page 64: Walt, ready to take Sharon to school in 1948. Diane and her classmates, Ann Middleton and Susan Zanuck, go along for the ride.

page 72: Detail from the original art for the poster pictured on page 75, promoting White Wilderness (1958), an Academy Award–winning True-Life Adventure.

page 76: Walt and fellow railroad buff Billy Jones, ca. 1948. Page 77: Walt's miniature home railroad, the Carolwood Pacific.

page 90: As this cartoon suggests, the death of Walt Disney was a loss felt around the world.

ILS No. F850-6835-5
288 2009

Printed on 100# Utopia Matte 30% PCW

preface

Walt Disney was a storyteller. Whether he was making a silent cartoon, a feature-length animated film, or a theme park, Walt was always telling stories. He worked with music, the visual arts, and cutting-edge technologies, but for Walt, these were merely tools used to tell stories. The story was king!

Walt received more than 900 awards for his artistic work and service to mankind, among them the *Chevalier de l'Ordre National de la Légion d'honneur* (1935), the Presidential Medal of Freedom (1964), and thirty-two Academy Awards®, including the Irving Thalberg Award. The Thalberg, given at the discretion of the Academy's Board of Governors to honor a creative body of work of consistently high quality, had previously been given to filmmakers near the ends of their careers. In 1942, at age forty, Walt was the fourth and youngest person to be so recognized. His work at that time consisted of cartoon shorts, the Silly Symphonies, and a few groundbreaking feature-length films, notably *Snow White and the Seven Dwarfs*, *Pinocchio*, and *Fantasia*. The rest was yet to come!

Yet the awards alone do not begin to tell the story of this man: the story of Walt the loving father and devoted husband, the friend and colleague, the artist and media mogul. Walt was all these things and much more—a man who was as simple and straightforward as he was complex and demanding, who was always working but always having fun. *The Walt Disney Family Museum* tells the story of Walt Disney: the man, the magic, and the memories.

—Richard Benefield
Founding Executive Director
The Walt Disney Family Musuem

introduction

My father discovered film animation in its earliest, most primitive form while working at the Kansas City Film Ad Company in 1920. He pursued it with a passion and carried it on to great heights, forming a company with his brother Roy. His other passion, discovered at an even younger age, when he moved from a rural Missouri farm to the bustling Kansas City of 1911, was the allure and excitement of amusement parks.

As long as I can remember, Dad talked about building an amusement park, and as the years went by, the dream grew. When Disneyland was finally realized, he found it especially rewarding, because it was something that he could keep improving, a living thing that would change with time, as the trees grew, and that he could change and improve as he wished.

That's the way we regard our museum. Dad himself narrates most of it, so he's a very strong presence in it. We will always be engaged in research and discovery, and will refurbish and add to our exhibits frequently. We offer programs that relate to his life and the things he found interesting. That gives us an inexhaustible number of choices, because he was interested in everything! This is a museum of his life, and it aims to reflect his spirit.

—Diane Disney Miller

1

beginnings

marceline kansas city red cross laugh-o-gram

Walter Elias Disney was born in Chicago on December 5, 1901, in a home his father had built. He was the fourth son of Flora and Elias Disney, who had been hoping for a daughter. His sister, Ruth, was born two years later, almost to the day. His brother Roy was eight and a half years his senior; their relationship was especially close. "He was always looking out for us, for Walt and me. He was full of fun, and always doing something for the family," Ruth recalled. Roy would become Walt's lifelong business partner, and was always his best friend.

> "My dad worked as a carpenter in Chicago on the World's Fair buildings. He worked for $1 a day, and out of that he and my mother saved enough money to go in business."
>
> Walt Disney

In April of 1906, the family moved from Chicago to a farm Elias had purchased in Marceline, Missouri. It was a beautiful farm and provided Walt with wonderful memories, peopled with extraordinary characters who all managed in some way to enrich his youth. Robert Disney was Elias's closest brother, and his wife, Margaret, doted on Flora and Elias's family, especially Walt. She would bring him Big Chief drawing tablets and crayons, encourage him, and praise his work. Walt's uncle Mike Martin, married to a sister of Flora's, was a railroad engineer who worked the route between Fort Madison and Marceline and often stayed the night with the Disneys. He would bring treats, and his visits were always looked forward to. Doc Sherwood befriended little Walt and encouraged his drawing. Erastus Taylor, a Civil War vet, told amazing stories

of his experiences and held Sunday concerts in his home, where Elias and another neighbor would play their fiddles, accompanied by the Taylors' daughter on the piano.

In spite of Elias's hard work, the farm did not provide a living, and in 1911 he moved his family to Kansas City, Missouri, buying a distributorship for the morning *Times* and the evening and Sunday *Star* newspapers. For six years, Walt would help his father to deliver papers morning and evening, in all kinds of weather. They had to rise early, to collect the papers at 4:30 in the morning. After the delivery was completed, Elias would go home for a nap, and Walt would go on to school. After school, he had the evening deliveries to take care of.

Above: Elias's brother, William Disney, was also a farmer. This is his farm in Ellis, Kansas. Opposite: Elias and Flora Disney.

In Kansas City, he discovered the magic of amusement parks, of moving pictures and vaudeville theater. He and Ruth attended the Benton School, and Walt, though an indifferent (probably sleepy) student, had a teacher, Miss Daisy Beck, and a principal, Mr. Cottingham, who would remember him, and whom he would never forget. He also had an important friendship with a boy who lived down the street, Walt Pfeiffer, who shared his interest in drawing and theater. The two of them often went to the theater together, and would devise skits to perform at school, coached by Mr. Pfeiffer, who loved theater himself and encouraged the boys to enjoy it. Elias Disney was of a different opinion, however, and Walt had to sneak out of his room at night to meet his friend for these entertainments. The Pfeiffer home was a warm, welcoming place for Walt, and this friendship would last for the rest of both of the boys' lives.

In 1917, Elias sold his route and moved to Chicago to become the supervisor of plant construction at the O-Zell Company, a jelly factory in which he had invested. Walt worked as a handyman for the factory, but sought other jobs as

well. He and Ruth attended McKinley High School in Chicago, with Walt joining the staff of the school magazine, *The Voice*, as its cartoonist and photographer. He also attended classes three nights a week at the Chicago Academy of Fine Arts.

In the late summer of 1918, Walt, like many young men of his time, was eager to join the military and get involved in the war, but he was too young. The American Ambulance Corps of the Red Cross was not strict about age, however, and needed drivers. Still technically a year too young, Walt was able to change the birth date of 1901 on his passport application to 1900. He was accepted, and finally embarked for France on November 18. He arrived at Le Havre on December 4, the day before his seventeenth birthday.

Opposite: "The Two Walts," Pfeiffer and Disney, in costume for one of their amateur-night performances. Above right: Walt drew numerous cartoons for his high-school magazine, *The Voice*.

His experience with the Red Cross lasted not quite one year, but it was an exciting, adventurous time of work and travel, and a rich source of memories and anecdotes for him. He returned home more mature in every way: physically taller and more worldly in outlook. Not content to stay in Chicago and work at the jelly factory, he returned to Kansas City, where Roy was living after his discharge from the navy. Roy was working at the First National Bank in Kansas City and planning to marry Edna Francis, sister of his longtime friend Mitch Francis. Walt's ambition at this time was to become a political cartoonist, and he hoped to find a job at one of the city's newspapers, but he was unsuccessful. Roy learned from a friend at the bank of two commercial artists who were looking for an apprentice. He told Walt, who hurried over to the Pesmen-Rubin Commercial Art Studio in the Gray Advertising Building. He was hired. He went immediately to tell his beloved aunt Margaret: "Auntie—they're paying me to draw!" But Margaret was dying and unable to understand what he was trying to tell her.

At Pesmen-Rubin, Walt met another artist his own age, Ubbe Iwwerks (the spelling of whose name was later simplified as Ub Iwerks). Both Walt and Ub were laid off at the end of the Christmas rush. After an unsuccessful attempt to start their own commercial art agency, they both went to work for the Kansas City Film Ad Company, which produced promotional films for local movie theaters. This proved to be a significant juncture in Walt's career, for it was here that he and Ub were introduced to the world of animated cartoons. Both were immediately fascinated by animation, and Walt learned more about it from two important sources: Eadweard Muybridge's photographic studies of human beings and animals in motion, and *Animated Cartoons* by E. G. Lutz, a recently published handbook that explained the basic principles of the art.

So taken with this new world was Walt that he began to experiment on his own. Most of Kansas City Film Ad's animated films were produced using jointed cutout figures;

Above: Walt in France. Note the cartoon on the side of his ambulance. Opposite: Walt at his Laugh-O-gram animation board.

> "We got books on animation and started to study."
>
> Walt Disney

this kind of film could be produced quickly and cheaply, but Walt soon tired of it. Hand-drawn animation, in which the drawing actually seemed to have a life of its own, was far more interesting to him. Borrowing a stop-motion camera from his boss, Walt built a makeshift camera stand in his garage at home. He began to produce a series of Newman Laugh-O-grams, short reels of advertisements and animated topical gags, for a local theater chain. These reels included both "lightning sketches"—vignettes in which Walt's own hand seemed to be sketching a detailed drawing at lightning speed—and some fully animated scenes.

Encouraged by the success of this experiment, Walt recruited Rudy Ising and a few other artists and started work on a one-reel story cartoon, *Little Red Riding Hood*, based on the traditional fairy tale but enlivened with Jazz Age gags. As it neared completion early in 1922, Walt's entrepreneurial spirit reasserted itself, and he established his first animation studio: Laugh-O-gram Films Inc. Walt's Laugh-O-grams were a series of modernized fairy tales, beginning with *Little Red Riding Hood*. The eager young artists learned and

refined their craft with each new film, and their cartoons took on a full range of gray tones and other effects.

But Walt and his staff, inexperienced in the ways of business, entered into an ill-advised contract with a distributor that was less than reliable. Soon Laugh-O-gram was in financial trouble, and Walt was tackling new projects in an effort to keep the little company afloat. One especially ambitious film, started in the spring of 1923, was *Alice's Wonderland*. This film began with a live-action story in which a little girl visited an animation studio—Laugh-O-gram's own office—and later, excited by what she had seen, dreamed her way into a cartoon world. Walt took a justifiable pride in *Alice's Wonderland* and began to write to potential distributors, including Margaret Winkler in New York, proposing an ongoing series of Alice films.

By the summer of 1923, however, it was clearly too late to save Laugh-O-gram Films. The little company declared bankruptcy. Walt, still buoyantly optimistic and carrying a print of *Alice's Wonderland* under his arm, boarded a train for Hollywood.

Opposite: Walt (left) and Fred Harman on location in Kansas City with the Universal camera, 1922. Above right: Lutz's *Animated Cartoons*, the handbook published in 1920.

2

hollywood

disney bros. ub iwerks alice comedies oswald

In the summer of 1923, Walt arrived in Hollywood and was taken in by his uncle Robert, who had relocated there with his new wife, Charlotte. Walt pursued his ambition to work in the movies, but openings at the studios were scarce, and he soon returned to his idea for a series of Alice Comedies. Margaret Winkler, on screening *Alice's Wonderland*, liked the concept and contracted to distribute a series of twelve pictures. On the night he received her telegram, Walt went straight to nearby Sawtelle Veterans' Hospital, where his brother, Roy, was recuperating, found his way to Roy's bedside, and proposed that they go into business together. Roy left the hospital the next morning, and in October 1923, the Disney Bros. studio was born.

"I came to Hollywood and arrived here in August 1923 with $40 in my pocket and a coat and a pair of trousers that didn't match."

Walt Disney

The Alice Comedies became Walt's first successful series and continued for the next three and a half years. The role of Alice was initially played by Virginia Davis (who had appeared in *Alice's Wonderland*) and then was taken over, in turn, by three other young actresses. The series continued to use the format of the first film: Alice would enter a cartoon world and interact with the cartoon creatures there, principally with a black cat who was eventually named Julius.

Walt, in shirtsleeves at left, directs Virginia Davis in a scene for *Alice's Spooky Adventure* (1924). Roy, at right, cranks the Bell and Howell camera. Above: Posters for two of the Alice Comedies.

At first Walt himself did all the animation for the Alice Comedies, but soon he began to recruit additional artists, notably Ub Iwerks and other friends from Kansas City. By the end of 1924, Walt had hired enough animators that he himself had been able to withdraw from animation altogether, the better to concentrate on direction and story work, at which he excelled. Among his other new employees was a lovely young inker named Lillian Bounds. A romance soon sprang up between Walt and Lillian, and in July 1925 they were married.

During the run of the Alice Comedies, Walt gained invaluable experience as a filmmaker and producer. His distributor, Margaret Winkler, married Charles B. Mintz in 1923, and Walt found himself corresponding regularly with the critical and sometimes hostile Mintz. But the Alice Comedies continued their modest popularity, and Walt's skill and confidence as a filmmaker grew steadily. In 1926 the Disney studio moved into new quarters on Hyperion Avenue. Over the next decade, the Hyperion studio continued to thrive, and in time it would become the birthplace of some of Walt's greatest films.

By 1927, Walt, feeling increasingly restricted by the demands of live action in the Alice Comedies, determined to end them and start an all-animated series. Oswald the Lucky Rabbit, a spunky, energetic new character, made his public debut in *Trolley Troubles* in July 1927 and quickly became a cartoon star. Distributed by a major studio, Universal Pictures, the Oswald cartoons were soon shown in bigger and more prestigious theaters.

But Mintz had been maneuvering behind Walt's back, and when Walt, traveling with Lilly, went east in February 1928 to negotiate a second Oswald contract, he was confronted with an unpleasant surprise. Mintz had secretly signed up most of Walt's animation staff and plainly expected Walt to give up his status as an independent producer and become an employee of Winkler Pictures. Instead, Walt relinquished both Oswald and the defecting animators. It was the latest in a series of hard lessons for Walt. From that point on, he decided, he would not deal with middlemen. He would create a new series starring a new character, and this time the Disney studio would retain full ownership of the character and the films.

Top left: Wedding picture at Lilly's brother's home in Lewiston, Idaho. Opposite, L to R: Mike Marcus, Lillian, Walt, Thurston Harper, Ub Iwerks, Ham Hamilton, and Roy outside the studio on Kingswell.

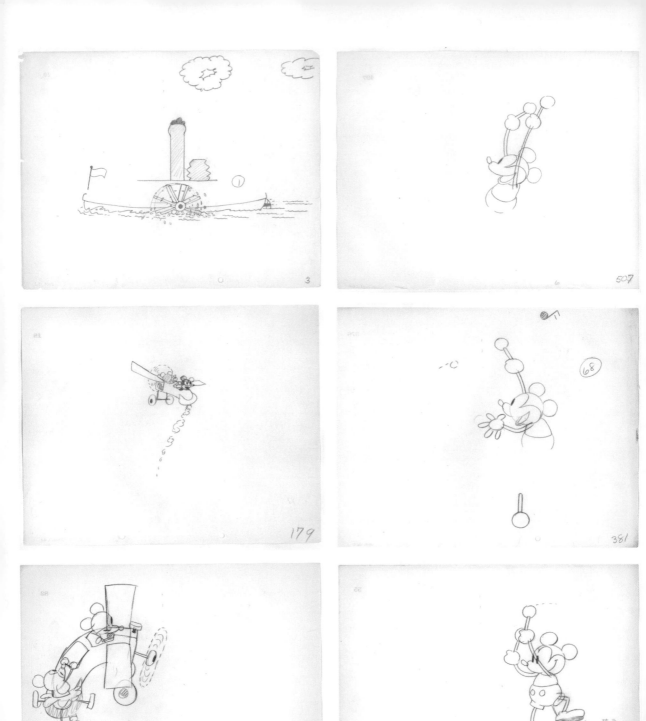

It all started with a mouse.

During the train ride back to California with Lilly, one of the most momentous events of Walt's career occurred: the birth of the character who would be christened Mickey Mouse. Ub Iwerks, who had remained loyal, worked with Walt to help develop the new character. The first two Mickey shorts were produced as silent pictures, but for the third entry, *Steamboat Willie*, Walt made the decision to join the talking-picture revolution and produce a sound cartoon. During the summer of 1928, he and his staff worked to produce their film, carefully tailoring it to fit a musical score with voices and sound effects. Then, armed with the score and the completed film, Walt returned to New York. Working with independent producer Pat Powers, he added a sound track to his cartoon.

Steamboat Willie opened on November 18, 1928, at the Colony Theater in New York and was an immediate hit. For Walt, it was the beginning of an extraordinary success story.

Opposite: Original animation art from the first Mickey Mouse cartoon, *Plane Crazy* (center and bottom left), and the third, *Steamboat Willie* (top left, all of right column). Above: These are believed to be the earliest drawings of Mickey Mouse.

3

new horizons in the 1930s

mickey mouse silly symphonies diane & sharon disney

The 1930s witnessed a phenomenal creative explosion at the Walt Disney Studio. Building on his success with Mickey Mouse, Walt immediately launched an additional series of cartoons, based on Carl Stalling's idea for a "musical novelty" reel. The result was the Silly Symphonies, an innovative series of one-reel shorts that began with *The Skeleton Dance* in 1929 and continued to appear for a full decade afterward. Unlike most cartoon series, the Silly Symphonies were not built around a single, continuing character, but introduced new characters in each picture. Unified (at first) only by their common emphasis on music, the Symphonies became an award-winning showcase for the art of animation. They brought a new level of prestige to the studio, and to animation itself.

Meanwhile, Mickey Mouse continued to flourish. The 1930s were Mickey's peak years—he appeared in his best films (his voice on the sound tracks provided by Walt himself), and also in a newspaper comic strip and an ever-increasing assortment of licensed character merchandise. Minnie Mouse, his sweetheart, had appeared in his earliest pictures and continued to thrive alongside him. Gradually more characters were added to the supporting cast: Pluto, a dim-witted hound; Dippy Dawg, a *humanized* dog who later evolved into Goofy; and a raucous, squawking duck named Donald. All these characters enjoyed a popularity of their own. In time, Donald Duck's popularity would surpass even Mickey's.

Behind the scenes, however, the Disney brothers experienced another serious setback when Pat Powers, their distributor and erstwhile benefactor, tried to take over their business. Early in 1930, Powers hired away Ub Iwerks and Carl Stalling, two key members of the studio staff. Walt and Roy quickly rallied, hiring new artists and musicians and severing their ties with Powers. Columbia Pictures, which was already distributing the Silly Symphonies, took over distribution of the Mickey Mouse series as well. (Later the Disneys would move to still more prestigious distributors: United Artists in 1932 and RKO Radio Pictures in 1937.) The Powers Cinephone sound-recording system meanwhile was soon replaced by the technically superior RCA system.

Left: The Disney characters were featured in a variety of storybooks during the 1930s. Opposite: Rough poster sketch for *The Bird Store* (1932).

Perhaps the most important Disney innovation of the 1930s was the art of personality animation—the expression of a character's personality through the way the character *moved*.

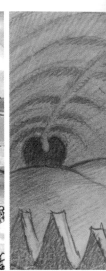

In one delightful, innovative cartoon after another, the studio transformed the face of animation. Among the studio's developments of the 1930s were:

COLOR. Walt had long wanted to produce his cartoons in color, but had been dissatisfied with the color processes available. The introduction of Technicolor's new three-strip process in 1932 finally provided the full, rich palette of colors he had been seeking. *Flowers and Trees*, a black-and-white Silly Symphony, was remade in Technicolor and caused a sensation in theaters, and soon all the Symphonies were being produced in color. Beginning with *The Band Concert* in 1935, the Mickey Mouse series also appeared in Technicolor.

Above and opposite, L to R: Story and concept art for *The Whalers* (1938), *Flowers and Trees* (1932), *The Whalers*, and *The Old Mill* (1937), and a French storybook cover for *Three Little Pigs* (1933).

DEPTH. Animated cartoons were commonly shot on a flat camera table, which was fine for most purposes but could not suggest three-dimensional settings. As Walt's cartoon world became increasingly elaborate, he sought a way to create a convincing illusion of depth in his films. The answer was the multiplane camera crane, a towering device that added greatly to the cost of production, but made captivating new effects possible. The multiplane made its public debut in a 1937 Silly Symphony, *The Old Mill*.

CHARACTER. Perhaps the most important Disney innovation of the 1930s was the art of personality animation—the expression of a character's personality through the way the character *moved*. The studio achieved a breakthrough in this area with *Three Little Pigs*, a Silly Symphony featuring three pigs and a wolf with distinct, appealing personalities. *Three Little Pigs* scored a sensational success in 1933 and was followed by more films featuring a gallery of engaging, memorable characters.

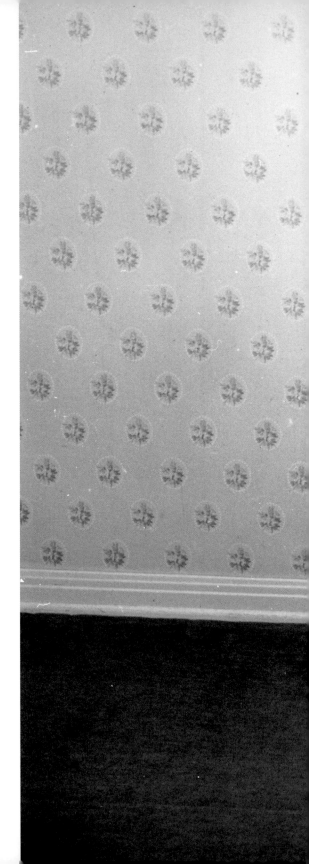

The 1930s were a decade of great personal and professional growth for Walt Disney. Privately, he and Lilly were blessed by the births of their daughters, Diane and Sharon. Professionally, Walt soared to new heights as he developed and refined the art of animation. His efforts were recognized and respected by Hollywood and the world: his films were honored with Academy Awards® and other tributes, and Walt himself was showered with distinctions, including honorary degrees from Harvard and Yale. As the decade drew to a close, it seemed that no goal was beyond his grasp.

Above: Walt, Mickey, and Roy with Mickey's special Academy Award® in 1932. Right: Walt with Sharon and Diane in Diane's bedroom in 1939, reading from *Pinocchio*.

"and i'll huff and i'll puff . . ."

Above and right: production art from *The Big Bad Wolf* (1934), the first sequel to *Three Little Pigs* (1933).

4

the move to features:
snow white and the seven dwarfs

snow white   hyperion studio   animation training

Having overcome so many of the perceived limitations of animated cartoons, Walt now challenged the limits of the one-reel short and set out to produce a feature-length film. For his story, he chose the traditional fairy tale "Snow White and the Seven Dwarfs." The production of *Snow White* (which Walt accomplished while still maintaining his output of Mickey Mouse and Silly Symphony shorts) would take four years and would prove one of the greatest challenges of his career. Some industry insiders predicted that it would fail disastrously.

This exciting venture reflected the restless, creative spirit that prevailed at Walt's Hyperion studio during the 1930s. As part of his preparation for the feature, Walt instituted a training program for the animators. Art instructor Don Graham was hired to teach a series of studio classes, focusing not on the making of static drawings, but on the study and analysis of movement. Walt insisted that his artists study live models and animals, not to *duplicate* reality in their animation, but to use it as a basis for convincing fantasy. Besides teaching the classes, Graham also helped recruit new artists for *Snow White*.

The training and the increased workforce were necessary, for this film offered the animators new and formidable challenges. The Seven Dwarfs represented an extreme exercise in personality animation: here were seven characters, all of similar height and appearance, each of whom had to be clearly distinguishable from all the others. Walt gave them names that

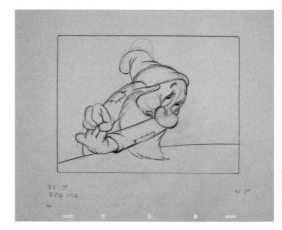

Right and opposite: Story sketches from the "Lodge Meeting" sequence, which was cut from the film, and an animation drawing of Snow White.

("I'LL FIX HER NAME")

expressed their personal traits, and, in numerous story conferences, worked with the artists and writers to develop a carefully delineated personality for each dwarf. In the finished film, the dwarfs emerged as seven distinct individuals. Snow White herself, along with the Prince and the Queen, presented an entirely different challenge: that of creating a convincing human character who moved in a believable way. Artists with expertise in human anatomy were assigned to these characters, and a young dancer, Marjorie Belcher, modeled for Snow White.

The key to the development of *Snow White* was the story. Walt was acknowledged by his staff as a master storyteller, and many of his artists remembered their introduction to the feature project: an evening meeting on the soundstage, during which Walt told the story of *Snow White* and acted all

the parts. In succeeding months he worked closely with the story department, adding new scenes, removing old ones, and refining the film's continuity. Walt maintained his focus on the overall arc of the story; some sequences that were entertaining in themselves—including a "Soup Sequence" that had already been animated—were removed because they did not contribute to the feature as a whole.

The finished film owed much to its music, which included eight songs by staff composer Frank Churchill. The songs were published in sheet-music form and issued in a special sound track record album, and some achieved success in their own right in the popular music market. This was only a small part of the film's publicity and promotion; a wide variety of *Snow White* books, toys, and other merchandise was marketed in coordination with the release of the film.

Above left: Publicity photo of Marjorie Belcher, who modeled for Snow White. Opposite: Production art and a cel setup from *Snow White*. The "Lodge Meeting" (top left) and "Bed-building" (center right) sequences were cut from the film.

SC 11
SEQ 11A

**UNIT
G**

4½F

ROTO

BASHFUL

HAPPY

**UNIT
G**

"All the Hollywood brass turned out for my cartoon! That was the thing, and went way back to when I first came out here and went to my first premiere. I just hoped that someday they'd be going in to a premiere of a cartoon."

Walt Disney

WORLD PREMIERE   2   Ward Kimball
Walt Disney's

"SNOW WHITE
AND THE SEVEN DWARFS"

Tue., Dec. 21, 1937
C A R T H A Y
C I R C L E

SPECIAL
"SNOW WHITE"
SUPPER MENU
$2.50 Per Person

✳

Stuffed Celery—"WITCH"
or
Fruit Cocktail—"QUEEN MOTHER"

✳

Choice of
Chicken Chow Mein—"DOPEY"
Chicken Chop Suey—"GRUMPY"
Welsh Rarebit—"DOC"
Lobster Newburg—"SLEEPY"
Chicken a la King—"SNEEZY"
Tenderloin Steak Sandwich—"HAPPY"
Chicken Liver Saute—"BASHFUL"

✳

Philadelphia Cream Cheese with Bar-Le-Duc—"PRINCE"
or
Special Ice Cream—"SNOW WHITE"

✳

Demi Tasse—"HUNTSMAN"

✳

Couvert $1.00 Per Person

The making of *Snow White* was recognized from the start as a risky venture, and in the closing months of production, as costs climbed to astronomical new heights, the risk became greater than ever. Walt was reluctantly persuaded to show the unfinished feature to Joe Rosenberg, of the Bank of America, who recognized the potential of this captivating film and extended the studio the necessary credit to finish it. In the end, Walt's gamble was vindicated on December 21, 1937, when the world premiere of *Snow White and the Seven Dwarfs* was held at Hollywood's Carthay Circle Theatre. An audience of hardened industry professionals embraced the film ecstatically, and Walt and his artists were reassured. Confounding the pessimists, *Snow White* went on to achieve an enormous worldwide success, and laid the groundwork for even more ambitious projects.

Opposite: Walt and Lilly arrive at the *Snow White* premiere. Left: A ticket from the premiere, and a special supper menu from that night.

5

"we were in a new business"

burbank studio bambi pinocchio sorcerer's apprentice

The success of *Snow White and the Seven Dwarfs* marked a profound turning point for Walt Disney. Freed from the financial restrictions that had bound him for so long, he was able to indulge his most ambitious ideas. In the summer of 1938, he and Roy started construction on a new, state-of-the-art studio in Burbank, California. As contrasted with the crowded, haphazard conditions that had marked the Hyperion Avenue location, the design of the new studio (by architect Kem Weber) afforded maximum comfort and efficiency for the making of animated films. By the spring of 1940 this beautiful facility was finished, and the staff had moved in. Some artists luxuriated in their new surroundings, but others felt increasingly isolated from the boss and from each other.

While the Burbank studio took shape, Walt and his staff were going ahead with the production of new and ambitious feature-length films. *Bambi*, based on the book by Felix Salten, had been started in 1937, even before the completion of *Snow White*, and for a time it was planned as the second Disney feature. But *Bambi* posed technical challenges that delayed its production. In particular, Walt and his artists were determined that the deer in the film should not be the cuddly cartoon deer of earlier pictures, but should convincingly represent real deer in the forest—while still retaining a full range of facial expressions. In extensive training sessions on animal anatomy, and through the study of live animals, both in captivity and filmed in the wild, the animators worked to achieve this goal. *Bambi* was not completed and released until 1942.

Meanwhile, the second Disney feature to emerge was *Pinocchio*, Collodi's story of the adventures of a living puppet. Maintaining the same high standard of character animation that had distinguished *Snow White*, this film added a new level of production gloss, and in particular, sophisticated effects animation: glistening highlights, rounded surfaces, and eerily atmospheric underwater scenes. In the end, *Pinocchio* became the most lavish, lovingly detailed animated feature in history, and one of the most expensive.

A cricket that had been a minor character in the book was transformed into Jiminy Cricket, one of the film's central characters, who served as Pinocchio's conscience. Show-business veteran Cliff Edwards found a second career as the voice of Jiminy Cricket.

Among the new Disney developments at this time was the Character Model Department. Headed by Joe Grant, this department produced not only model sheets but actual three-dimensional models of major characters. By turning these models, the animators could instantly see how the characters looked from any angle. New technical developments, too, proliferated, including refinements to the original multiplane camera. Eager to take full advantage of this device, the artists pushed it to the limit of its capabilities. Some "multiplane" scenes became so elaborate that even the standard multiplane cranes could not accommodate them; instead, they were filmed on horizontal tracks on the soundstage.

Above: Walt with animator/director Ham Luske.
Opposite: Story sketch from *Pinocchio*.

48

"We don't actually make films for children.
We make films that children can enjoy along with their parents."

Walt Disney

"Walt was really imbuing all of us with something that made us feel that we were part of a renaissance in the animated cartoon business."

Mel Shaw, animator

As Walt's prestige continued to increase in the late 1930s, prominent artists and writers sought him out. Some, like Alexander Woollcott and Frank Lloyd Wright, were invited to lecture at the studio; others, like Oskar Fischinger, actually worked on Disney films. Walt's casual conversation with conductor Leopold Stokowski led Stokowski to participate in producing a unique short, *The Sorcerer's Apprentice*, starring Mickey Mouse and set to the original Paul Dukas score, played by a full orchestra. This in turn developed into another strikingly ambitious Disney feature, *Fantasia*, with eight classical compositions illustrated by means of animation. The music for this groundbreaking feature was performed by the Philadelphia Orchestra, conducted by Stokowski and recorded via an innovative stereophonic sound process dubbed Fantasound. Walt hoped to exhibit *Fantasia* in concert halls and to continue to produce new segments for it.

Unfortunately, his plans were scaled back after the film's disappointing box-office reception. For most of its exhibition life, *Fantasia* would be shown in theaters with a standard sound track. Compounding the disappointment, none of these subsequent features duplicated the spectacular worldwide success of *Snow White* during their initial releases. The war in Europe, which was expanding into a world war and effectively closing the European film markets to American producers, significantly reduced the returns on these films. And the war and other events would continue to alter Walt's course during the early 1940s.

Opposite: Deer study by Marc Davis for *Bambi*. Above left: A life sketching class for the *Bambi* artists. Above right: George Balanchine, Igor Stravinsky, and Walt with a *Fantasia* model and storyboards, December 1939.

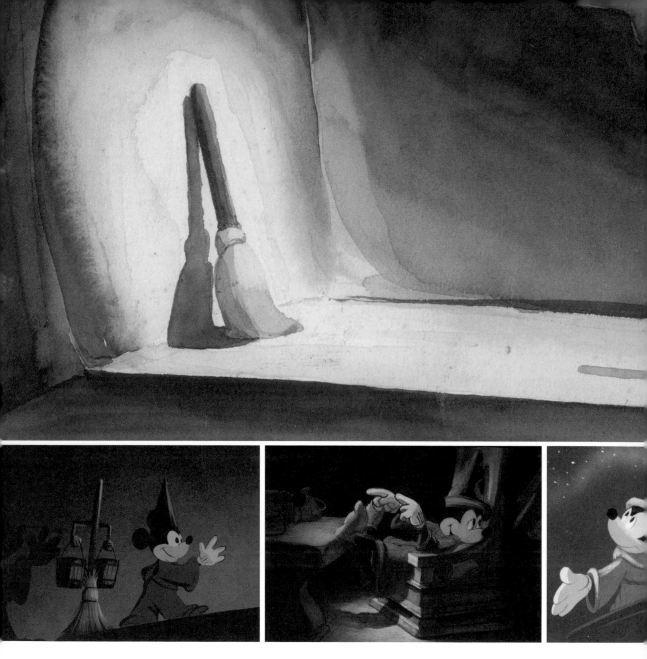

Above and opposite: Story art from *The Sorcerer's Apprentice*, which was originally planned as a special Mickey Mouse short but evolved into the feature-length *Fantasia*.

The unnamed sorcerer in *The Sorcerer's Apprentice* was nicknamed
Yen Sid ("Disney" spelled backward) by the Disney artists.
Leopold Stokowski suggested the title *Fantasia*, which literally means
"A medley of familiar themes, with variations and interludes."

6

"the toughest period in my whole life"

1941 disney strike world war II dumbo el grupo

As the 1930s ended and the 1940s began, Walt was assailed by personal and professional crises. The deaths of his parents—first Flora, in November 1938, then Elias, in September 1941—were personal losses that moved him deeply, but which he kept carefully hidden from the outside world. Meanwhile, at the studio, an artists' strike erupted in the spring of 1941. Labor unrest had been brewing in American industry at large, and early attempts to unionize the Disney artists had led to a dispute between competing factions. Preliminary talks between the studio and the artists were unsuccessful, and on May 28, a group of the artists walked out. Walt initially believed that the strike would be settled quickly, but instead it dragged on for months.

Eventually—after the intervention of a federal mediator and a period of several weeks during which the studio closed its doors altogether—the strike was resolved. But by that time the damage had been done. The strike would remain a painful crisis in Disney studio history, creating bitter divisions among former friends that would not soon be forgotten. Walt's own clear memories of the ordeal, and his conviction that the strike had been Communist-influenced, resurfaced six years later as he testified before the House Un-American Activities Committee (HUAC).

Along with these events there was a truly global crisis: World War II. The war's impact on Walt and his studio was immediate: on the same day Pearl Harbor was attacked, army units charged with protecting the nearby Lockheed plant moved into the Disney studio in Burbank to use it as a base. The war would also effect a marked change in the studio's production. Some theatrical features were already in progress; *Bambi*, for example, with its complex animation challenges, would not be completed

Above: At the family home shortly after Flora's death. Seated, L to R: Elias, Ruth Disney, Dorothy Disney Puder. Standing, L to R: Walt, Lilly, Charlotte Disney, Jessie Call Perkins (Flora's sister), Robert Disney Jr., Robert Disney Sr., Glen Puder, and little Diane. Opposite: Two of the many Armed Forces insignia designed by Disney artists during the war.

★ ★
SEASON'S GREETINGS *1943* U.S.S. HOUSATONIC

> "Little *Dumbo* was one that we had a lot of fun with. That film was the most spontaneous thing we've ever done."
>
> Walt Disney

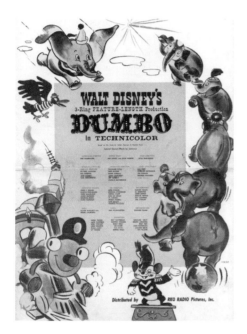

Opposite, above, and overleaf: Story sketches and a trade ad for *Dumbo*.

and released until August 1942. In the meantime, Walt, mindful of the box-office losses incurred by expensive epic films like *Pinocchio* and *Fantasia*, had also started a more modest feature, *Dumbo*. Released in October 1941, *Dumbo* represented a return to the Disney studio's basic strengths: strong storytelling and compelling character animation. It was a critical and financial success, and remains today one of the best-remembered Disney classics.

With the entry by the U.S. into the war, however, the studio's production underwent a radical change. Walt contracted to produce a series of training films for the military; his public-service shorts for theatrical showing included *The New Spirit*, which encouraged Americans to pay their income taxes and support the war effort, and *Out of the Frying Pan into the Firing Line*, which promoted conservation. Another war-related production was an unusual feature called *Victory Through Air Power*, based on the book by Alexander de Seversky, which Walt undertook as a personal initiative because he believed in Seversky's ideas. Among the Disney propaganda cartoons during the war years was *Der Fuehrer's Face*, which won the Academy Award® for Best Short Subject of 1942. The studio's wartime efforts also included nonfilm activities, among them the creation of hundreds of insignia, at no charge, for various branches of the military.

 One activity only indirectly related to the war was Walt's participation in the government's Good Neighbor program, which was designed to promote friendly relations between the U.S. and the countries of Latin America. In 1941, Walt and a group of his artists, nicknamed El Grupo, agreed to conduct a tour of South America, forging bonds of goodwill even as they gathered their visual and musical impressions of Brazil, Argentina, and other countries. Returning to the studio, they distilled those impressions into two feature-length films, *Saludos Amigos* and *The Three Caballeros*, along with a variety of short subjects for both theatrical and educational showing.

All these endeavors tested Walt's and the studio's strength, but the end of the war in 1945 brought challenges of a different kind. During the turbulent years of the strike and the war, Walt had drastically revised the organization of his studio, and almost all of his production had been war-related. Now he and Roy found themselves with reduced resources, and suddenly operating without the government contracts that had sustained them for several years. Thanks to the loyal support of A. P. Giannini, the Bank of America agreed to extend their loans; but they knew that somehow they must rebuild their business.

Above: An evocative South American painting by Mary Blair, a member of El Grupo; and cover art for the *Saludos Amigos* record album. Opposite: Walt with the gauchos in South America.

7

postwar production

studio rebuilding lady and the tramp 20,000 leagues

Walt and Roy met the challenge of the postwar years by diversifying their production. Before the war, the Disney studio had been established as the unquestioned world leader in animation; during the war they had ventured into live-action production and gained experience in unfamiliar forms of filmmaking. Now all that experience would be harnessed and used in new ways to rebuild the Disney program of theatrical films.

> "Our re-conversion job consists of reorganizing our staff, of training others to provide for increased production, and to build up our inventory of stories in preparation and of pictures in work. All these qualities mean good pictures, and good pictures mean that our future is assured. We have a clear road ahead. Let's get on our way."

Walt Disney, from Annual Report, December 31, 1945

Walt was in no hurry to resume production of expensive animated features, partly because of the studio's weakened financial condition, but also because he instinctively resisted repeating himself. He much preferred to try new ideas. The Disney backlog of cartoon stories included numerous ideas that fit no convenient category; they exceeded the scope of one-reel shorts but were not substantial enough to sustain a feature. One strategy was to combine an assortment of these stories in a package feature. The first such feature, *Make Mine Music*, was released in 1946 and was followed by *Melody Time* in 1948. Each offered a colorful variety of animated segments, linked by their emphasis on music and featuring sound track performances by such guest stars as Dinah Shore, Benny Goodman, and the Andrews Sisters. A variation on this idea was to combine two featurette-length stories in a single feature, as in *Fun and Fancy Free* (1947) and again in *The Adventures of Ichabod and Mr. Toad* (1949).

Another outlet for animation was to combine it with live action, as Walt did in two films with a strong flavor of rural Americana. *Song of the South*, based on the Uncle Remus tales, was essentially a live-action film, punctuated with animated interludes that illustrated Remus's stories. *So Dear to My Heart*, built along similar lines, was a film with deeply personal associations for Walt: its story of a boy and his pet lamb depicted turn-of-the-century farm life and reflected something of Walt's own childhood.

Opposite: Sheet-music cover from *So Dear to My Heart*. Above: A lobby card advertising *Fun and Fancy Free*.

All of these films were modestly successful, but it was clear that the public really wanted more Disney features like the great prewar classics. Inevitably, Walt bowed to popular demand. As his fortunes improved in the late 1940s, he resumed production of several animated features that had been started before the war. *Cinderella*, completed and released in 1950, was a great success and was followed by *Alice in Wonderland* and *Peter Pan*. Along with these adaptations of literary classics, Walt produced a dog story, based partly on original Disney material and partly on a contemporary novel. The result was the delightful *Lady and the Tramp*, the studio's first wide-screen animated feature.

Left: Original concept art by Mary Blair for *Peter Pan*. Above: Scenes from *Cinderella, Lady and the Tramp,* and *Alice in Wonderland*.

Meanwhile, one of the Disney brothers' postwar problems pertained to "frozen" funds: specifically, box-office revenue that had been earned in England during the war but could not be taken out of the country. Walt's solution was to use the money to produce films in England. In doing this he completed his move into the role of live-action film producer; these overseas productions were adventure stories with no element of animation. The first, *Treasure Island*, was released in 1950 and was followed by *The Story of Robin Hood* and other action adventures. These films achieved some modest success and led in turn to a far more ambitious live-action picture: *20,000 Leagues Under the Sea*. This was a huge production, filmed domestically and on location in the Bahamas, and starred some of the most prominent actors in Hollywood. Released in 1954, it was immensely successful and established Walt in no uncertain terms as a producer of live-action films as well as animation.

Top: Robert Newton as Long John Silver in *Treasure Island*. Center: Advertising for *The Story of Robin Hood*. Bottom: Captain Nemo (James Mason) in trouble in *20,000 Leagues Under the Sea*. Opposite: Poster art for Walt's most ambitious live-action film to date.

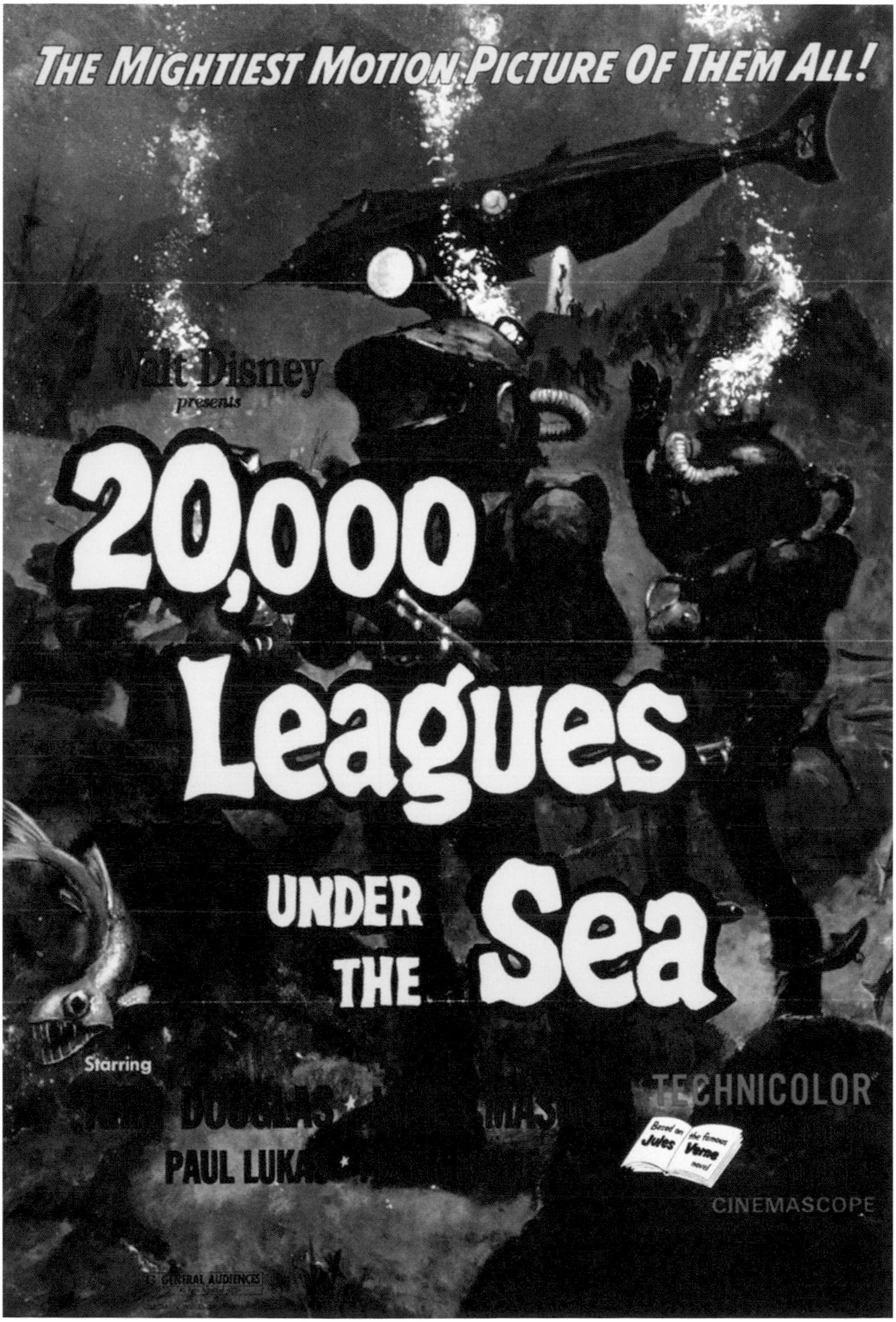
THE MIGHTIEST MOTION PICTURE OF THEM ALL!
Walt Disney
presents
20,000 Leagues UNDER THE Sea
Starring
PAUL LUKAS
TECHNICOLOR
Based on the famous Jules Verne novel
CINEMASCOPE
GENERAL AUDIENCES

8

walt and the natural world

true-life adventures seal island people & places

One of the most unusual highlights of Walt's career was a series of nature documentaries, the True-Life Adventures. The first of these films grew out of an experiment: Walt hired Alfred and Elma Milotte, a husband-and-wife cinematography team, to shoot a quantity of film in Alaska. When some of the Milottes' film revealed fascinating scenes of the seals in the Pribilof Islands, Walt shelved the rest of the footage and edited the seal material into a short subject that documented the seals' life cycle on the islands. *Seal Island* became the first True-Life Adventure, enjoying a successful theatrical release in 1949 and winning an Academy Award®.

Seal Island set the pattern for the series: Walt would hire a team of cinematographers to spend months or years in the field, shooting scenes of wildlife; then his team would edit the hours of resulting footage down into a theatrical film. These films presented unique technical challenges. The cinematographers, shooting in unpredictable conditions in the wild, used lightweight and portable 16 mm cameras and strong telephoto lenses to capture nature's wonders. Their 16 mm film stock was prone to surface scratches, but Ub Iwerks, who had returned to the studio, devised a "liquid gate" that removed the scratches when the film was blown up to 35 mm.

The result of all this work was an innovative kind of nature documentary. Many of the naturalist/photographers who contracted with Walt had previously conducted lecture tours, illustrating their talks with the films they had shot, but the True-Life Adventures were professionally produced, with the resources of a major motion-picture studio.

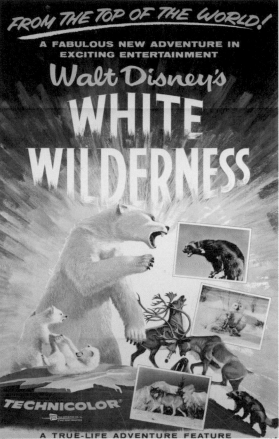

They offered an authentic screen record of the world of nature, presented in an entertaining package that informed and delighted theater audiences. The series continued through the 1950s, enjoying continued success and winning numerous awards. The first feature-length True-Life Adventure, *The Living Desert,* appeared in 1953 and was such a success that six more features were produced.

Building on this success, Walt launched a second documentary series, called People and Places. Beginning in 1953 with another Alaskan subject, *The Alaskan Eskimo,* the People and Places shorts continued through the rest of the decade and were similarly successful, garnering multiple Academy Awards® of their own.

Opposite and above: Posters for a selection of True-Life Adventures, including the short subject *Bear Country.* Center left: Al and Elma Milotte, the husband-and-wife team who photographed many of the films in the series.

9

the 1950s and 1960s: the big screen and beyond

trains disneyland **television** the florida project

As the 1950s dawned, Walt Disney stood on the threshold of yet another phase of his career. His motion-picture studio was busier than ever, working on both animated and live-action films, but Walt was looking for new worlds to conquer.

TRAINS. One major new activity began as a hobby: Walt's fascination with railroad trains—scale models as well as the genuine article. In 1948, Walt and fellow railroad buff Ward Kimball traveled together to the Chicago Railroad Fair. Both men thoroughly enjoyed this huge event, featuring displays of vintage and modern locomotives, and it served to reawaken Walt's long-standing interest in trains.

DISNEYLAND. During their 1948 visit to Chicago, Walt and Kimball made a side trip to Greenfield Village, a public display of antique buildings that Henry Ford had assembled near Dearborn, Michigan.

Besides his interest in trains, Walt developed another hobby around this time: collecting and building miniatures. This pursuit soon developed into a plan to build miniature dioramas, representing different periods in American history, in a traveling exhibit.

Gradually all these interests came together in Walt's mind, combined with his ambition, conceived as early as his Kansas City years, to build an amusement park that might entertain adults as well as children. By the early 1950s he was actively developing such a park. As his plans became more ambitious, he formed a private company, WED (for Walter Elias Disney), for this and other personal projects.

Opposite: Walt with daughter Diane and grandson Christopher in one of the Autopia cars at Disneyland. Above: Before the park's opening, Walt describes his plans for Disneyland.

In 1955, Walt's new park opened to the world as Disneyland. Utterly unlike existing amusement parks, Disneyland was designed as a fresh, inviting world unto itself. It was divided into four "lands":

Tomorrowland, which celebrated the new wonders that science was discovering and would continue to discover; Fantasyland, dominated by familiar scenes and figures from the fantasy worlds Walt had already created on the screen; Frontierland, summoning up the excitement and color of frontier days, when the pioneers were settling America; and Adventureland, built around a Jungle Cruise in which guests traveled by boat into a mysterious jungle.

These "lands" radiated like spokes from a hub at the center of the park. Leading, in turn, from the park entrance to the hub was Main Street, U.S.A., a nostalgic re-creation of small-town America at the beginning of the twentieth century.

Walt commented on many occasions that, unlike a motion picture, Disneyland would never be finished. He could continue to tinker with it indefinitely, "plussing," improving old attractions, and adding new ones. True to his promise, Disneyland has continued to evolve to this day.

TELEVISION. In the late 1940s and early 1950s, many motion-picture producers looked on broadcast television as a new threat that would lure audiences away from theaters. Walt, instead, embraced the new medium. He and Roy arranged a deal with ABC: the network would invest in Disneyland, and Walt would produce for them a weekly series, also titled *Disneyland*. The series premiered in October 1954, with Walt himself as the weekly host. Like its namesake, the *Disneyland* series revolved around four themes: programs associated with Adventureland highlighted the True-Life Adventures; programs from Fantasyland featured new and classic Disney animation; Tomorrowland presented a series of award-winning programs on man's exploration of space; Frontierland produced one of Walt's major successes of the 1950s—three episodes of the adventures of frontiersman Davy Crockett, starring Fess Parker in the title role. So successful were these programs that they sparked a nationwide Davy Crockett craze. Walt produced two more Davy Crockett episodes for the television series; later, all these episodes were reedited into two feature-length Crockett films and released in theaters.

Above: Opening title sketch from "Davy Crockett—Indian Fighter," which aired on the *Disneyland* series in 1954.

"SPACE TOOLS"

"HOMO SAPIENS EXTRATERRESTRALIS"

"ACTION...REACTION"

NEWTON

This was possible partly because, even though the television standard of the time was black-and-white, Walt had the foresight to produce these and other episodes in color.

In 1955 Walt launched another successful television series: the weekday children's program the *Mickey Mouse Club*. In this program a cast of youngsters, the Mouseketeers, entertained a nationwide audience their own age with songs, newsreels, serials, and Disney cartoons. The *Mickey Mouse Club* attracted a fanatical following and enjoyed a long run.

More TV triumphs followed, including another series, *Zorro*, starring Guy Williams, which premiered in 1957. *Disneyland* continued its successful run, retitled *Walt Disney Presents* in 1959 and *Walt Disney's Wonderful World of Color* in 1961.

Top: Sketches for "Man in Space," a 1955 episode of *Disneyland*. Above right: The official logo of the Mickey Mouse Club.

MOTION PICTURES. Meanwhile, Walt's motion-picture enterprise, the backbone of his company, grew stronger than ever. Walt greatly expanded his program of live-action production in the mid-1950s, with further adventure yarns as well as warm family dramas like *Old Yeller*, *Toby Tyler*, and *Pollyanna*, and some unclassifiable gems such as the charming Irish fantasy *Darby O'Gill and the Little People*. He also launched a series of live-action comedies, including *The Shaggy Dog* and *The Absent-Minded Professor*, filled with sight gags and usually starring Fred MacMurray.

And Walt's animation division, the foundation of all his success, remained the world's premier animation studio and continued its celebrated output.

After years of delays, *Sleeping Beauty* finally appeared in 1959, distinguished by a highly stylized design scheme and a musical score adapted from Tchaikovsky. More features followed: *One Hundred and One Dalmatians*, with its experimental visual style, and *The Sword in the Stone*.

BEHIND THE SCENES. While all these events were taking place in Walt's public life, his family was growing. Diane had married in 1954, and Sharon five years later. By now, Walt and Lilly had two sons-in-law, and eventually became proud grandparents of seven. The family enjoyed occasional relaxation time at a vacation home Walt had built at Smoke Tree Ranch in Palm Springs, California.

Opposite: Atmospheric concept art by Eyvind Earle for *Sleeping Beauty*. Above: Diane and Sharon join Lilly and Walt in celebrating their thirtieth anniversary, a few days before the opening of Disneyland.

FURTHER EXPLORATIONS. Meanwhile, Walt continued to explore new horizons. After staging the opening ceremonies for the 1960 Winter Olympics at Squaw Valley—an ambitious undertaking in itself—he took on an even greater challenge: four major Disney attractions for the 1964 New York World's Fair. These attractions were developed at WED by the same Imagineers who had planned Disneyland. The four attractions were: the Illinois Pavilion, featuring a life-size, lifelike Abraham Lincoln in Great Moments with Mr. Lincoln; the Pepsi-Cola Pavilion, which introduced It's a Small World; the Ford Pavilion, with a panoramic view of history along the Ford Magic Skyway; and the General Electric Pavilion, highlighting the benefits of electricity in the GE Carousel of Progress.

All these attractions benefited from a sophisticated new WED technology called Audio-Animatronics, in which figures were controlled not mechanically but electronically, their movements programmed as a series of signals on magnetic tape. At the end of the fair, most of these attractions were shipped back to California and reassembled at Disneyland.

THE FLORIDA PROJECT. Following the World's Fair, Walt and Roy began to plan a permanent new Disney park on the East Coast. Settling on a site in Florida, they laid the plans for what would become Walt Disney World in Orlando. The new park would duplicate some of the attractions of Disneyland, but Walt was far more interested in new ideas. At the heart of his vision was the Experimental Prototype Community of Tomorrow, or EPCOT. Walt visualized this as both an experimental laboratory and an actual working community, in which temporary residents could experience the latest ideas in electronics, utilities, and transportation in their everyday lives. He believed that this might have an impact on the quality of life throughout the rest of the country and the world.

Walt Disney World was eventually completed after Walt's death, and it did feature a component called Epcot—but Walt's original vision was never realized.

Far left, top: Walt demonstrates a model of It's a Small World. Center: Mary Blair concept art for It's a Small World. Above right: Walt describes his plans for the Florida Project.

MARY POPPINS. One of the last important projects of Walt's life was a motion picture produced on a grand scale. For *Mary Poppins*, Walt utilized all the resources of his studio: live action, animation, music, and cutting-edge special effects.

The resulting film was wildly successful. Julie Andrews, making her film debut, inhabited a magical screen world that could only have been created at the Disney studio. *Mary Poppins* won five Academy Awards®, including one for Julie Andrews as Best Actress—and was nominated for many others, including Best Picture.

Above left: A story sketch for the film. Right: Julie Andrews with Walt for a *Mary Poppins* publicity photo.

FINAL PROJECTS. In the final months of his life, Walt Disney and his studio were still hard at work on a variety of projects. Along with a full slate of television and film production—both animated (*The Jungle Book*) and live-action (*The Happiest Millionaire*)—Walt continued to explore new horizons with his characteristic zest. The Florida Project was being actively developed, and in the meantime he had launched additional projects: an ambitious, interdisciplinary art school, and an environmentally innovative ski resort at Mineral King Valley. The art school would eventually be completed, greatly revised from Walt's concept, as California Institute of the Arts; the Mineral King project would not be realized at all. But Walt himself continued to embrace life as enthusiastically as ever, working on new projects to the end.

Right: A scene from *The Jungle Book*, the animated feature that was still uncompleted at the time of Walt's death.

10

december 15, 1966

Walter Elias Disney died·on December 15, 1966, ten days after his sixty-fifth birthday, in St. Joseph's Hospital—directly across the street from the studio that he and his brother had built in Burbank, California. The nation and the world reacted in grief and disbelief, and condolences came to his family and his company from all over.

'--But We Live Happily Ever After'

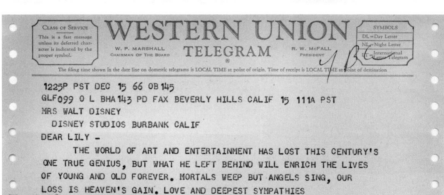

1225P PST DEC 15 66 OB 145
GLF099 O L BHA143 PD FAX BEVERLY HILLS CALIF 15 111A PST
MRS WALT DISNEY
    DISNEY STUDIOS BURBANK CALIF
DEAR LILY —
    THE WORLD OF ART AND ENTERTAINMENT HAS LOST THIS CENTURY'S
ONE TRUE GENIUS, BUT WHAT HE LEFT BEHIND WILL ENRICH THE LIVES
OF YOUNG AND OLD FOREVER. MORTALS WEEP BUT ANGELS SING, OUR
LOSS IS HEAVEN'S GAIN. LOVE AND DEEPEST SYMPATHIES
Mr. + Mrs. FRANK AND LUCILLE CAPRA

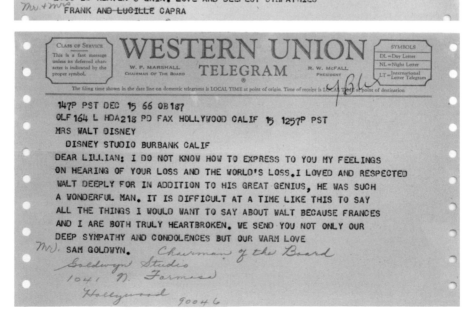

147P PST DEC 15 66 OB 187
OLF 164 L HDA218 PD FAX HOLLYWOOD CALIF 15 1257P PST
MRS WALT DISNEY
    DISNEY STUDIO BURBANK CALIF
DEAR LILLIAN: I DO NOT KNOW HOW TO EXPRESS TO YOU MY FEELINGS
ON HEARING OF YOUR LOSS AND THE WORLD'S LOSS. I LOVED AND RESPECTED
WALT DEEPLY FOR IN ADDITION TO HIS GREAT GENIUS, HE WAS SUCH
A WONDERFUL MAN. IT IS DIFFICULT AT A TIME LIKE THIS TO SAY
ALL THE THINGS I WOULD WANT TO SAY ABOUT WALT BECAUSE FRANCES
AND I ARE BOTH TRULY HEARTBROKEN. WE SEND YOU NOT ONLY OUR
DEEP SYMPATHY AND CONDOLENCES BUT OUR WARM LOVE
Mr. SAM GOLDWYN. Chairman of the Board
Goldwyn Studio
1041 N. Formosa
Hollywood 90046

His brother Roy led the company in continuing the projects Walt had begun. The Mineral King project, which had been enthusiastically approved by California's governor Pat Brown and the U.S. Forest Service at the time of Walt's death, was defeated by the Sierra Club in a lawsuit that went as far as the Supreme Court. The concept of EPCOT, the Experimental Prototype Community of Tomorrow, was revised; it became World Showcase and Future World, the reasoning being that the realization of the "city of the future" was heavily dependent on Walt's own vision and direction. The acronym, however, was kept, and EPCOT Center ultimately became Epcot.

The California Institute of the Arts was built in 1969 on a hill overlooking California's Interstate 5. The School of Animation was added by the Walt Disney Studios in 1978, and was staffed entirely by veterans of the Disney animation department. John Lasseter, a member of the first graduating class and a founder of Pixar Animation Studios, became the head of Disney Animation.

Roy Disney declared that Disney World, the Florida project that lived so vividly in Walt's imagination, that he had begun but never seen realized, would be named *Walt* Disney World, so that everyone would know it was Walt's creation. Roy's energies, fueled by his love and grief for his younger brother, saw both CalArts and this second theme park through to completion. Roy, with Walt's widow, Lillian, dedicated Walt Disney World on its opening day with these words:

Walt Disney World is a tribute to the philosophy and life of Walter Elias Disney . . . and to the talents, the dedication, and the loyalty of the entire Disney organization that made Walt Disney's dream come true. May Walt Disney World bring Joy and Inspiration and New Knowledge to all who come to this happy place . . . a Magic Kingdom where the young at heart of all ages can laugh and play and learn—together.

Roy O. Disney, October 25, 1971

Roy Oliver Disney died in St. Joseph's Hospital on December 20, 1971.

Opposite: Newspaper cartoonists, and Walt's Hollywood peers, expressed the world's grief at his passing.

the museum campus

The Walt Disney Family Museum was built to tell the story of Walt Disney while adapting old, historic buildings for entirely new use. Three structures comprise the museum, forming a recognizable "campus within a campus" at the Presidio in San Francisco.

The permanent galleries of the museum are located at 104 Montgomery Street (Building 104), one of five identical barracks buildings dating from the 1890s that flank the west edge of the Main Parade

Ground. To accommodate the exhibits and better facilitate circulation, a 20,000-square-foot addition was designed to occupy the U-shaped barracks courtyard. This addition—a glass-and-steel pavilion—is very distinct from the brick masonry structures that surround it, and it connects to wings on three floors. A theater with state-of-the-art screening capabilities occupies the lower level of the pavilion, adjacent to an education center with two studios for teaching digital animation and traditional art techniques.

Offices for both the museum and the Walt Disney Family Foundation are located at 122 Riley Avenue (Building 122). Built in 1904, the building was originally the army post gymnasium. The central space was restored for use as a special exhibition hall. A small building constructed in 1940 for machine-gun storage now houses the physical plant for the museum campus.

Opposite: The Rockwell Group's rendering (Luis Blanc, illustrator) of Gallery 9. © Rockwell Group, LLC. Above: Page & Turnbull's renderings (Chris Grubbs, illustrator) for the special exhibition hall in Building 122, and the rear of Building 104 showing the glass-and-steel pavilion. © Page & Turnbull, Inc.

Architect
Page & Turnbull

Interior Architect and Exhibit Design
Rockwell Group

Project Management
D. R. Young Associates

Contractor
Plant Construction Company, L.P.

Exhibits
Kubik Maltbie, Inc.; Goppion; BBI Engineering, Inc.; Kerner Optical; EffectDesign, Inc.; Techifex, Inc.; Second Story; Roto Studios

Media Production
Batwin+Robin Productions, Inc.; Tarrigo, Inc.

Museum Consultant
ISG Productions

Content Consultants
Bruce Gordon, J. B. Kaufman, Jeff Kurtti, Paula Sigman Lowery

Research Consultants
Hugh Chitwood, Jennie Hendrickson